Henry Tate.

Park Hill.
Streatham Common.

For Alvie, Ted and Ramona

First published 2015 by order of the Tate Trustees by Tate Publishing,
a division of Tate Enterprises Ltd, Millbank, London SW1P 4RG.
www.tate.org.uk/publishing

A catalogue record for this book is available from the British Library
ISBN 978 1 84976 169 7

Distributed in the United States and Canada by Abrams, New York
Library of Congress Control Number applied for

Designed by Graphic Thought Facility
Colour reproduction by DL Imaging
Printed in China by Toppan Leefung Printing Ltd

HENRY TATE

Bruce Ingman

Tate Publishing

**This is Henry Tate
and this is his story.**

When Henry Tate was a little boy
he was always busy.
He loved growing things.

And selling things.
Henry was very clever.

It wasn't long before he had his first shop.
And then another and another.
Soon he had six shops.

He delivered his vegetables far and wide.

The next thing Henry Tate did was
to build a sugar factory.
He made lots of sugar cubes
and a lot of money.

He also made horses very happy.

Then Henry's life changed forever.

One day, on his way home, he saw the most beautiful painting.

**That was just the beginning.
He loved paintings so much he
started collecting them.**

He loved going to art galleries.
He went to more than you could ever imagine.

He bought even more
paintings and sculptures.

Soon his home was filled with beautiful pictures.

Henry Tate was a kind man. He wanted to share his collection of paintings and sculptures.
He knew it would make people happy to come to his house to see them.

Henry was right.

HENRY'S
ART GALLERY

People loved visiting so much
they didn't want to go home.

Ever!

Henry knew what to do.
He would find a big home
for his collection so
everyone could enjoy it.

He wrote to the biggest art gallery in the land to
offer them his collection of paintings and sculptures.

If the big gallery didn't have room,
he would just have to build his own.

So that was exactly what he did.
And if you go to London today you can
visit Henry's gallery.

Henry

HENRY
TATE'S
GALLERY